Bucky's Adventures

Marjorie Cox Gray

Written by Marjorie Cox Gray,
Illustrated by Marlin Griffin

Marlin Griffin

Bucky

AuthorHouse™
1663 Liberty Drive, Suite 200
Bloomington, IN 47403
www.authorhouse.com
Phone: 1-800-839-8640

First published by AuthorHouse 2/2/2009

ISBN: 978-1-4389-2645-2 (sc)

Printed in the United States of America
Bloomington, Indiana

This book is printed on acid-free paper.

authorHOUSE®

Dedication

"BUCKY'S ADVENTURES" are dedicated, as a gift of love and happy memories, to my son Hugh Edward ("Buck") Gray and my husband, his father, Edward Leonidas "Buck" Gray who also shared these memories.

Also, to my parents - Jennings Masceo Cox and Miriam Catherine King Cox who taught me to always give one hundred percent plus to any endeavor.

They also instilled in me their love of nature and to never forget to take care of it and its contents.

Marjorie Cox Gray

1

Preface

Dear Buck:

When you were very little, I used to make up bedtime stories, we called adventures, and do primitive sketches of the characters and when I say primitive, I mean VERY primitive.

Interestingly, last year one of the many adventures, "TAB THE CRAB" surfaced, and it brought back so many good memories. This adventure was the only one done in rhyme; the others are in story form. I had hoped to have this one printed and given to you for Christmas. After showing "TAB THE CRAB" to several current and former teachers, the consensus was that I try to remember some of the other adventures and have them published so that they could be shared.

After contacting a friend and well known illustrator Marlin Griffin, I ask if he would consider being the illustrator of the adventures. He said, "YES"! The next step was to seek the expertise of a friend, Jim Chitwood, the Executive Director of the Northwest Florida State College Foundation, Niceville, Florida whose guidance has proven invaluable in moving forward with this endeavor.

The time had arrived to share with you the findings and what Mom wanted to do with some of Bucky's adventures.

You were so pleased that they could be shared and brought up to this era as the Cox-Gray family has always cared about the protection of our environment.

Love, Mom

Special Thanks To

Marlin Griffin for his wonderful illustrations and for allowing his beautiful, caring character Mermaid Crystal Clear, to appear in your dreams in "Bucky's Adventures". Marlin has some fascinating illustrations and stories to share with Mermaid Crystal Clear so watch for their publication.

Paula, Pam and Sheryl, friends known as the D'Vine's, an outstanding trio, for allowing me to use their names as the dolphin trio. They truly fit the description of the word divine.

Jimmy Weathers for allowing me to use him as one of the characters to help tell the story of Boggy Bayou.

Norma Walker Anderson, Polly Barnes, Charlotte Flynt and Elva Scholes for their evaluation and proof reading plus being my cheer-leaders. Also, to the many other cheerleaders; you know who you are and I thank each of you.

It is now time to explore, learn, and dream through "Bucky's Adventures".

Contents

1

Tab The Crab

Here, at Choctaw Bay and the Beach,
when school was out,
children would yell and run about.
But a younger little boy named Bucky Gray
was curious and liked to sometimes stray.
He would seek out creepy and crawly things
and sometimes suffer bites and stings.

He has a pet with furry paws,
but none with big red snapping claws.
I had seen this little boy down by the Bay and shore
but never knew his name before,
until his mom called out one day -
Bucky, Bucky, Bucky Gray.

I sort of liked the little tot,
In fact I liked him quite a lot.
When he was by the Bay,
he'd toss bread crumbs and scraps my way!

Then one quiet and sunny day I saw
 a shadow over me.
I thought this might be Bucky,
Could I be so lucky?
He really looked the same..and yet….
he had a pole and a fishing net.

12

Bucky had some fish heads and meat,
just the things crabs like to eat.
He dropped a morsel down to me,
I did not see the string you see.
My claw reached out to grab the bait.

I had no cause to fear or fret
'til I was tangled in his net.
Up, up, I came so slowly,
and quickly sprung the net.

Alone, so sad, I was placed in his pail,
but down came my tears with a big wail.
He then explained, to me, just how
safe I would be.
Somehow, I knew no harm would come
'cause I believed Bucky would become my chum.

I must have been his strangest pet,
he gave me water and snow white sand
and gently held me in his hand.
Now, I could have snapped and hurt this little boy,
but to him I was his pride and joy.

He was so proud of what was in his hand.
He rushed back to show me to his Mom and Dad.
Bucky said, "He looks quite sad and needs to
be back with his friends and Mom and Dad".

As time went by they all could see
that this pail really was not for me.
Bucky was so good and kind to me
but he understood my home was in the Bay or sea.

As morning dawned, Bucky grabbed my pail,
and swiftly headed down to the pier by the Bay trail.

As soon as I could go SNAP, SNAP
I would know that I no longer was in a trap.
Bucky clapped his hands and I snapped mine
and suddenly I was back in the water
and things were just fine.

He waved goodbye, smiled and shed some tears and called to me to never fear.

Now, I am back in the sea, but I stay a lot in the bogs
with minnows, shells and chirping frogs.
They tell me that I've changed somehow
and that I am not as CRABBY now.

I, Tab The Crab, must admit that I was very lucky
that summer day when I met BUCKY.

2

Mermaid Crystal Clear Takes Bucky On A Treasure Hunt

"Goodnight, Bucky, we love you and we hope that you have pleasant dreams...."

"It is so beautiful here in Bluewater Bay at Sunset Beach. I love playing in the snow white sand while looking across Choctawhatchee Bay to Destin. Oh, there are some pelicans on the posts and they are all sizes!"

A deep-voiced pelican speaks up and says, "Yes, Bucky, we come in many sizes. We love the Emerald Coast, Choctawhatchee Bay and the Gulf of Mexico. We would love to show you around some time."

"How exciting! I would really like that, but how did you know my name?"

"Tab The Crab, told us to look after you."

"I miss Tab. What is your name?"

"I am known as Scoops The Pelican."

30

"Glad to meet you, Mr. Scoops The Pelican!"

"Bucky, did you know that Choctawhatchee Bay is named for the Indian Tribe that lived here as early as 10,000 years ago? Most of us refer to it as Choctaw. It is shorter and easier to say and for you to spell too. All of us pelicans have also been around for a long time and are known as Brown Pelicans. I'm called the old man of the group. There is safety in numbers so we travel in groups.

I know that you had to notice our straight long bills with large pouches attached. Our pouches hold three times what our stomachs can hold. We dive and catch fish and keep them in the pouches to feed the young. Also, it keeps us cool. That is like having our own air conditioning unit! Did you notice my wing span? It is 7½ feet long. Some only have 6½ foot wing spans. Watch me soar! WHEEEEEEE……..."

"Did you see Mermaid Crystal Clear, sunning herself on the boat?"

"Oh, my goodness, a real mermaid!"

"She is motioning for you to come over. She wants to meet you."

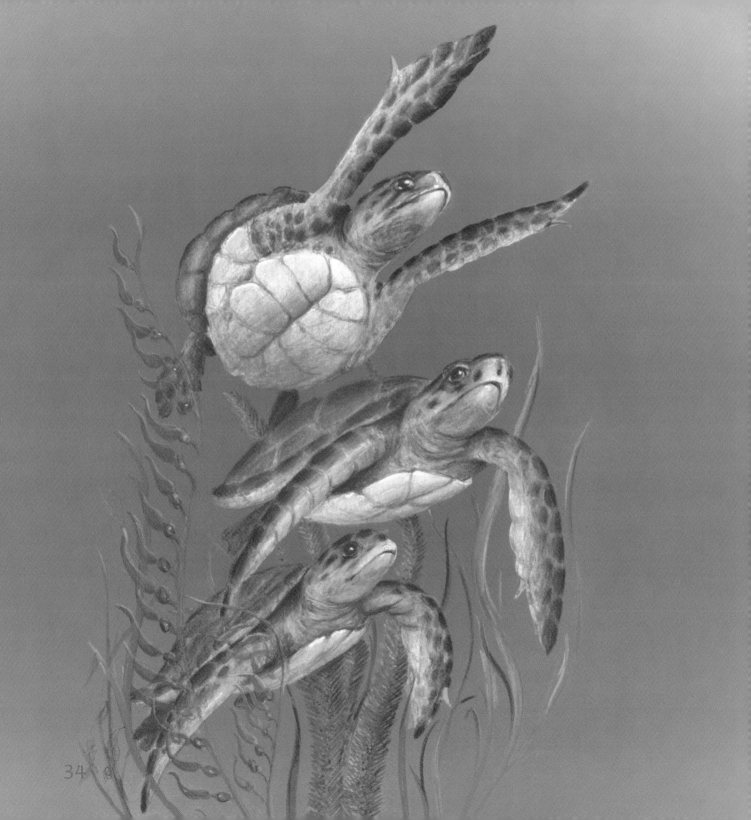

34

"Hi Bucky, I am Mermaid Crystal Clear. Tab The Crab said I should take you treasure hunting. Would you like to go today? I have a scuba diving outfit for you, and we can practice before starting our trip around the bay and the gulf. There are lots of our friends who want to meet you because you care about us and want to keep us safe. Glad you got to meet Scoops. He is one of the older pelicans and full of wisdom."

"I would love to travel with you, Miss Crystal Clear."

"I believe we are now ready to greet and meet some of your new friends and start the treasure hunt."

"Look, Bucky, there goes Elmer, Delmer and Selma, our turtle friends. They are waving at us."

"Hi Bucky, would you like to hitch a ride with us?, said Elmer. If so, hop on Delmer and I will lead the way. Selma will be right behind us."

"Bucky, there are a large number of us turtles around the Emerald Coast. We are known as the Green Sea Turtles and vary in size from around 31 to 44 inches in length and our weight is quite large. Old timers can weigh over 400 pounds. I have been around a long time, but my Granddaddy is 80 years old. And here is something interesting, Bucky. For some reason, we cannot retract our heads into our shells like the land turtles."

"What do you mean that you cannot retract your head in to your shell?"

"Retract means we cannot pull our head back in to our shell."

"Thank you but I want to mention something else to you. My Dad said he read where a large green sea turtle washed up on shore, and it is believed it died from a plastic bag it had swallowed."

"Carelessness like throwing plastic bags on shore that can blow into the water or left on shore can be very harmful to us as well as other treasures of the sea and land. Tell your friends to be careful."

"I will Elmer and thank you again. You too, Delmer and Selma!"

"Well, it looks like Delmer and Selma wants to move on and look for food, but we WILL meet again."

"Miss Crystal, you said we would go treasure hunting. Have you ever seen a sunken ship with treasures?"

"Yes, I have seen a sunken galleon (that is a large ship) and on a _future trip_ we WILL visit a small ship in the Gulf of Mexico. You have seen some of the REAL treasures of the bay and gulf today. Your treasures are the coral and all the wonderful species of fish and birds."

"What is a species, Miss Crystal?"

"Species - hmmmmm, let me think of an easy way to explain species. Take a look at the seagulls above and note that they all have the same characteristics as to mannerisms and appearance. The pelicans and dolphins are another example."

"To keep all of the species safe, it is important to protect the environment."

"How do you say that word, N-VI-RO-MENT?"

"At a future time, we will ask Environmental Annie, who lives close by, to do a "show and tell" about how important this is for you and your friends."

"O.K. Will I see you again soon, Miss Crystal?"

"YES, you will, Bucky. When you go to bed, just close your eyes, fall asleep, and perhaps you will dream. I promise to be there to continue your treasure hunt. There is SO much more to be shared. Sweet dreams, little one!"

3

Sally Seagull & Mermaid Crystal Clear Treasure Hunt Again

"Psst...Bucky, it's Mermaid Crystal Clear. I am here in your dreams again and it's time to meet some more friends - our treasures - here in Choctaw Bay and the Gulf of Mexico."

"First, let's stop on the beach and let you feed the seagulls.
Oh, look there is Sally Seagull and with her are Dolly and Polly."

"Bucky, would you like to soar with Dolly, Polly and me? We will show you some treasures of the shore and meet some other friends."

"I would like to do that. Goodbye for now, Miss Crystal."

"As we sail along, Bucky, let me tell you a little about seagulls. Aren't we just beautiful!"

"The three of us are considered large gulls, but we can vary from small to large. Some gulls can be as little as 4.2 ounces and 11.5 inches wide up to our size which is 3.8 pounds and 30 inches wide. It takes us, depending on size from 2 to 4 years to become an adult."

"And...if I were not flying with you, I would dive down now and catch that crab and these little fish. We like live food but also enjoy other foods - we are considered to be very intelligent and resourceful and protective of each other if predators come close. Something I bet you did not know is that we drink salt and fresh water. Most animals cannot do that! Sometimes I think we are sort of lazy because we do not venture real far out to sea. We love being close to the shore. When I see you fishing, I will show you where to cast your line so you can catch a fish. Our beaches are beautiful with all this snow white sand!"

"Oh, there is Teddy Flounder and near by is Miss Crystal awaiting you with your scuba outfit. She wants you to meet some new friends….some more of the real treasures of the bay and gulf. Have fun."

"Thank you, Seagulls Sally, Dolly and Polly. I learned a lot today and will watch for you and have some bread ready."

"Bucky tell your friends to cut the plastic pieces around their cold drinks into small pieces and safely discard them to help protect us.....it is easy for birds and animals to get their bills, necks and feet caught into them and die."

"I sure will Miss Sally and thanks for showing me the beautiful Emerald Coast and Choctaw Bay from above."

"It is time to head into the bay and gulf, Bucky. Well, here we go and let's head to the jam session."

"Wow, a jam session!"

"We are here! There is Octy Octopus playing the piano. Paula, Pam and Sheryl, the singing dolphin trio and Simpy Shrimp just arrived with a trumpet. Let's stay awhile and enjoy their music. Oh, there goes a school of fish."

"I didn't know fish went to school too!"

"Well, they don't exactly. That is just a term used when they travel in groups behind their leader; they are learning from their leader. It is also safer to travel in groups."

"Octy Octopus can really play that piano."

"He should - he has 8 arms! Also, a lot of suction cups. Let me tell you more about octopuses while we listen to Octy play the piano. Octopuses love to be around coral reefs, and if predators come around, they can eject (that is shoot out) a black ink like that forms a cloud to protect themselves. Did you know they only live a few months and have 3 hearts? There are 300 known species and for some unknown reason a group in the Northern Pacific can live up to five years. Research has shown the octopus to be highly intelligent. Now, let's just relax and listen to Octy play that piano, the girls sing and Simpy blow his trumpet. I believe I will join them and play my harp in a few minutes."

"We think the dolphin trio is divine. Their names are Paula, Pam and Sheryl. Would you like to know more about dolphins, Bucky?"

"I sure would but what does trio and divine mean?"

"Trio means three. Divine means inspiring, godly and great."

"Well, that is what they are. You know where I live in Bluewater Bay at Sunset Beach, I love to watch the dolphins play in the bay. We can sit on our little beach and four miles or so across the Choctaw Bay we can see Destin. Tell me some more about dolphins."

"Dolphins are marine mammals and are closely related to whales and porpoises. Marine means water. There are about 40 species and believe to have been around for over 10 million years."

"Ten million years - WOW. We have so many wonderful species here on the Emerald Coast. It is so exciting and interesting. I love all of them and we ARE going to protect them and our environment. Tell me more, Miss Crystal."

"Dolphins are different shades of grey with a little lighter color underneath. They are from around 4 feet to 30 feet in size and eat lots of fish and squid. They are considered among the most intelligent mammals plus being playful and friendly but very protective of each other. Some of their faces look like they are smiling with their curved mouth."

"Recently I heard they have up to 250 teeth which are placed in a way that they receive sounds like an antenna. This might account for their outstanding hearing ability, far greater than we humans. There have been reports of how they have saved human lives with their protective abilities."

"My Mom and her friend, Dixie, got in the water with the trained dolphins at our nearby Gulfarium and the dolphins did all kinds of tricks with special signals they had been taught.

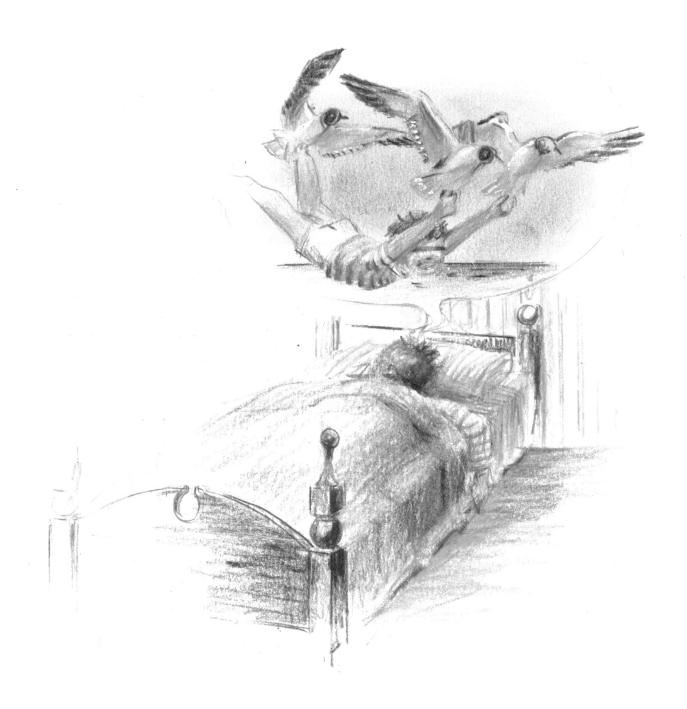

Mom also got to rub one and said their skin was so soft and one dolphin even held her hands and kissed her on the cheek."

"That was a great experience for your Mom. When you are a little older and taller, I bet your Mom and Dad will take you to play with the trained dolphins. Now, wave goodbye to Octy, the girls, and Simpy as it is time to head home."

"Now close your eyes and finish your dreams precious one. I will see you again soon…in your dreams…to find more treasures. Night, Night."

4

Bucky & 'Little Man' Travel Around Boggy Bayou & Another Treasure Hunt

"Hey Mom and Dad, 'Little Man' and I are heading out to see what is going on and since 'LM' is such a 'couch potato', we are taking my little red wagon."

"What a beautiful Blue Heron 'LM' and he is right here in our yard. He has long legs and neck and a long tapered bill. I have seen him here at Sunset Beach before. He must be living in the marshes nearby. I know they build their nests around April and May. Let's roll along and see what other of nature's treasures that we can see."

"See those bushes over there, 'LM', my Mom saw what she thought was a coyote the other night. It is hard to be sure, but they are in the area and are a part of the wild dog family. They really look a lot like a small wolf so we have to be careful. We better move on."

"Hi Isabella, want to tag along? We are looking for nature's treasures."

"Yes, I sure would like to tag along. May I ride in your red wagon?"

"Join us, but not in the wagon right now…that is 'LM's' territory! And, since I just mentioned territory, we sure do live in a beautiful area called Bluewater Bay. My parents keep telling me that we should call this area a "paradise" because of its beauty, its people and its variety of activities on land and water."

"Hummmm, I know a LOT about this area."

"O.K., Isabella, so start talking …. Smarty."

"I like everything about nature - even bugs, spiders, lizards, snakes and frogs! AND….I also learned about the history of this area. My kindergarten teacher told me."

"Well, don't keep it a secret. I want to know, too."

"Let us just call this DID YOU KNOW THAT…..   .
Native Americans were living here up to 10,000 years
ago. Have you ever visited the Museum in Fort Walton
Beach? There was fighting among the Native Americans and
European explorers between 1500-1700.

- Archaeologists now believe that the horrible hurricane
  that hit in September, 1599 and destroyed a number of
  ships in Pensacola Pass may have discouraged further
  exploration from the water until 1698.

- Archeologists also have found some Aztec artifacts in
  the sunken ships in the Pensacola Pass and are now
  studying areas in Mexico to learn more about those
  individuals who were on the ships.

- Native Americans also conquered some Spanish
  conquistadors and pirates.

Maybe we should go treasure hunting for pirates' gold! I
remember those stories because it was so exciting and
interesting. I bet my teacher would be proud that I could
remember that much."

"Lots of mullet are jumping out there in the Bay and there are Jimmy and his dog, 'Sadie', she is a Chihuahua. Jimmy loves to fish, hunt wild turkeys and knows a lot about this area. He grows great big juicy tomatoes plus he is a great story teller."

"Little Man, shake hands with Mr. Jimmy. 'LM' is 6 years old and was just recently adopted from an animal shelter in the Charlotte, North Carolina area. Since we do not know his birthday we decided celebrate on the 4th of July."

"Mr. Jimmy, this is my friend, Isabella, and I told her you could tell us about this area. Do you have the time?"

"You bet and I really like to talk about our beautiful area so let us get started. In the 1800's, settlements and trades were getting started and one was the fishing industry. There are lots of mullet in this area - we have sandy bottoms in our bay which is good for fishing. Our bay area was called Boggy Bayou. With fishing being so good, villages started being developed."

"We like the name Boggy Bayou, Mr. Jimmy."

"That was the original name of Niceville. If it had not been changed in 1910, you would be living in Boggy Bayou. In came cattle and some settlers and it was becoming pretty settled by the end of the Civil War.

Some people were still unhappy about the name so in 1919 it was changed to Valparaiso. Do you know what that means?"

"No, but it sounds Spanish."

"Isabella, you are correct it is Spanish and means, 'Vale of Paradise'. However, due to a lot of confusion with the post office and others in 1925, the name of Niceville was restored. Now, about where you both live. In January, 1976 there were 1,500 acres purchased for development and the area was named Bluewater Bay which resulted in many diverse neighborhoods and businesses. That is another story for another time, but I will tell you that the planning was and is a role model for other areas due to being protective of our environment. Your mail is delivered as Niceville, Florida in Okaloosa County. Guess I better get back to taking care of my friends and get in a little fishing before sundown. Thanks for wanting to learn more about your community."

"Thanks, Mr. Jimmy and 'Sadie'. Isabella, 'Little Man' and I are going to head home. Nap time! Race you to the couch, 'LM'."

"Psst...Bucky, it is Mermaid Crystal Clear, I promised to return to your dreams and show you a sunken galleon. Let's head out in to Choctaw Bay and the Gulf of Mexico and I will share some more information about the area."

"We are in the Bay now - Choctaw Bay's freshwater feeds from a number of creeks and rivers and then connect to Pensacola and East Passes thru the Destin Pass - that is about 50 miles or so."

"I have a question, Miss Crystal Clear. I hear people say let's go over to the ocean, but we call it the Gulf. I do not understand."

"Actually, Bucky, the Gulf of Mexico is not the ocean.

It is the 9th largest body of water in the world and is a BASIN of the ocean. The Gulf of Mexico is surrounded by the North American Continent to the Island of Cuba. It is pretty big, almost an oval basin!"

"WOW...but it sure acts like the ocean with all the waves rolling in. The water along our beaches are what my parents call emerald green. Guess that is why it is called the Emerald Coast."

"We are getting pretty far out now in the Gulf and nearing a sunken ship. I say ship because when we say galleon, that is considered a large ship. Here we go ....and there she is - a very old small ship."

"Where are the treasures?"

"All sunken ships do not hold treasures of gold and artifacts of value. But let's swim around and feel the old wood and see if we can find anything. Oh, that looks like a little piece of broken pottery."

"I wish we knew the story of what happened, don't you."

"Yes, I do. Each one would have a very special story about what happened and about the people who were on the ship."

"Look at the pretty fish going by, Bucky. Remember what I told you about treasures in one of your earlier dreams......the REAL treasures are the wonderful species in the water and on the shore."

"I remember and you also told me to always be protective of them and our environment."

"It is time to head home now and back to your other dreams. I wish for you a happy life and many more wonderful dreams and opportunities.

Take good care of our environment. Perhaps you can be one of the leaders to remind people how important it is to do so.

It is now time for me to return to Marlin Griffin's Mermaid Village so this is a farewell. Good night, precious friend."

5

Environmental Annie
Has Show & Tell Time

"Hi Bucky, I am Environmental Annie. Our friend, Mermaid Crystal Clear, told me to visit with you and tell you more about how you and your friends can help keep the environment safe. Since a small octopus just washed up on shore would you like see it up close before we get started? I understand you have already learned a lot about octopuses."

"Sounds like we are going to have Show and Tell Time today. These are my friends John and Isabella. Donna and Steve are coming up the beach now."

"Nice to meet you. I brought my large easel board and marker so I can show you some of the things that can cause problems. Oh, look above you! There goes a bald eagle! It is classified by the State of Florida as a threatened species."

"I know what that word species means, Miss Annie. And, I also know that if a species is threatened, it means we must protect them."

"Well, Bucky, since we have just seen a bald eagle fly over head let me tell you a little more about them.

They are a large, dark brown bird. Also, they have a white tail and head and their eyes, bill and feet are yellow."

"His wings looked mighty big, Miss Annie."

"Isabella, they are indeed large and their wings can spread from about 6.5 to 8 feet, but it might not be a he, it could be a girl. The female is usually larger than the male."

"Since they are so big, do they make great big nests?'

"Oh yes, Steve, and they are built with sticks about five feet long and could be up to around 100 feet from the ground."

"But how big?"

"Oh, Steve, I did forget to tell you how big! I did not know until recently when I read in the NW Florida Daily News that a bald head eagle's nest is 4 - 5 feet wide!"

"Miss Annie, my Mom and Dad took me on a helicopter ride in Alaska, and we saw some bald eagles from above and their heads looked like light bulbs all lit up."

"How true, Bucky, and we are also able to see them right here in the Panhandle of Florida. We were so lucky this morning, to have a bald eagle fly over-head. They are beautiful and a symbol of our nation's freedom. In fact, they are our national bird."

"While up in the helicopter in Alaska, we also saw a mama bear and her two babies. Oops, I meant cubs. My parents said they are called cubs."

"Interestingly, people are surprised to learn that we have bears here in the Panhandle, as well as in other areas of Florida. They are black bears and most are 'ear-tagged' or wear a radio collar so that they can be studied by wildlife organizations, such as the Florida Fish and Wildlife Conservation Commission and some universities. Bears from time to time venture into neighborhoods looking for food. The reason is that our population is growing and extending into what was formerly their territory."

"You mentioned, Bucky, that you saw a mama bear with her cubs and you are probably right. A mama bear stays with her cubs until at least the second summer of their life. At this time they become known as yearlings. Black Florida bears live to an average of 15 years and have been known to live to be 30. The males can weigh between 250 - 450 pounds while the female is between 125 - 250 pounds. They are large, powerful animals that eat animals and plants as their food. The North American bears have been here for at least 1.5 million years."

"How fast can they run, Miss Annie?"

"Bears shuffle, but can travel up to 30 miles per hour, John, and can climb trees."

"Our black bears are a little different than others - they have a highly arched forehead, long narrow brain case area, rounded ears, short tails and five-toed feet. Well, that is enough about black bears right now."

"Now…let's share some other important information on protection of our precious environment. First, let's talk about various items that are often thrown into the bay, gulf, and rivers and even left on shore."

"How many of you recycle cans, glass bottles and papers at your home?"

"Wonderful! All of your hands went up and that is 100 percent. Congratulations to you and your families for doing the right thing."

"Since we are here on our beautiful beach, let's have our 'Show and Tell', all about water debris timetables. Some of the timetables will be quite shocking. Give me some examples of things you have seen thrown into the water."

"Plastic bottles."

"John, this is one of the shockers - it takes 450 years for a plastic bottle to dissolve."

"Milk cartons and newspapers."

"The waxed milk cartons take 3 months and the newspapers 6 weeks Steve."

"Isabella and I saw some cans floating in the bay yesterday."

"We see this quite often, Donna, and there are two type of cans - tin and aluminum. The tin can takes 50 years and the aluminum 200 years to dissolve. Hearing these large number of years tells us that re-cycling is important, as it keeps some items out of the water and off the shore or left on shore. Plus they can be put to good use again."

Sally Seagull said the plastic six pack rings can injure and kill our fish, birds and animals."

"She is correct, Bucky, the plastic ones take 400 years to dissolve. That is a long time and can injure or cause the death of many of our treasures. There are some pack rings called photodegradable (that is a big word) that dissolve in 6 months, but this is still not acceptable for our environment. We need to cut these rings into many pieces before we put them in the garbage or the trash."

"How do you know about these timetables, Miss Annie?"

"This information is available in your schools, the college, the Internet and many other organizations that have an interest in our environment and marine life. And, don't forget about our local library. One of the best ways to educate others is by word of mouth - that is talking with your friends and by your actions."

"But, how do they know how long it takes to dissolve?"

"This took a lot of research in labs all over the world. The labs have equipment to test various objects, Isabella. That was a good question. In fact, all your questions today are very good. This is how you learn."

"John, Steve and I like to fish. How about fishing lines?"

"There are so many different kinds of fishing lines but research has shown it takes up to 600 years to dissolve, Bucky."

"WOW, we better not leave any in the water or on the shore. Do styrofoam cups disintegrate right away? We use lots of cups and paper towels, too."

"Styrofoam cups are bad news - they take up to 50 years and the paper towels, 2 - 4 weeks. None of you have mentioned food being tossed into the water. An apple core is an example. It takes two months to dissolve."

"Hey, Miss Annie, we have some visitors. I think they are called sandpipers."

"They are indeed sandpipers, Steve. These tiny birds are so cute and fast. They look like little gulls and are looking for food."

"Look! There are some shrimp boats out in the distance. Shrimping is quite popular in this area and we have bay shrimp and gulf shrimp. They have a similar taste, but their color is slightly different."

"I have a few more minutes to share with you and if there is another question I will be happy to try to answer it."

"Miss Annie, I have one more - how about diapers I see people throwing overboard from their boats?"

"That is a real problem, Donna. People often start out on their trips without planning a safe way to dispose of waste. Sadly, research has shown that it takes 450 years for a disposable diaper to dissolve in the water. There are some special diapers that are biodegradable (that means they have been specially treated) that takes 1 year. Either way it is not good to dispose of diapers in the bay or gulf or anywhere."

"It has been such a pleasure and so much fun to be with you today and to see your enthusiasm about protecting our environment."

THANKS FOR CARING !!

"Thank you, Environmental Annie, we have learned a lot today and we will continue to care and tell our friends. But, look far out into the Gulf. I think there are some of my 'dream friends' waving to us with a banner flying across the sky...what does it say?"

It is a real important message for everyone -

THANKS FOR CARING

THE END?

WHY NO....it is just the beginning....
START NOW TO PROTECT OUR ENVIRONMENT!

What I Am Going To Do
To Protect Our Environment!

_____

_____

_____

_____

_____

_____

_____

_____

_____

_____

My Drawings

Draw some pictures of things you should not throw into the water or leave on the shore.

About the Author

Marjorie Cox Gray, since childhood has always been known as visionary and caring. She spent most of her life in Charlotte, North Carolina moving to the Florida Panhandle (Bluewater Bay-Niceville) in 1996, following her husband's death.

In each of her home areas, and in Houston, the author was an active community leader as she felt strongly one should give back to their community. Marjorie, despite being a woman of the late 1920's was able to wear many hats professionally - nursing, teaching, administrative positions, developing new concepts, writing, sought after motivational speaker and retired as a Senior Communications Specialist with Exxon Company, U.S.A -Hdq/Houston, with 31 years of service.

She loved telling her son, Buck, stories….several became this book - "Bucky's Adventures".

About the Illustrator

Marlin Griffin's artistic flair spans from still photography, to painting, but he enjoys pencil drawing the most. Throughout the years Marlin has served as a combat cameraman, owned several advertising agencies and has traveled most of the world documenting his travels with his talent. His published works includes Life Magazine and National Geographic. Marlin resides in Bluewater Bay - Niceville, Florida.

His talented works can be found in many homes and galleries and when presented in art shows are often voted to be the favorite of those attending. Marlin has a passion for fantasy drawings.

Thank you Dad and Mom for
CARING and sharing our memories.

Love, Bucky

Printed in the United States
138630LV00002B